The books in the Here's Hank series are designed using the font Dyslexie. A Dutch graphic designer and dyslexic, Christian Boer, developed the font specifically for dyslexic readers. It's designed to make letters more distinct from one another and to keep them tied down, so to speak, so that the readers are less likely to flip them in their minds. The letters in the font are also spaced wide apart to make reading them easier.

Dyslexie has characteristics that make it easier for people with dyslexia to distinguish (and not jumble, invert, or flip) individual letters, such as: heavier bottoms (b, d), larger than normal openings (c, e), and longer ascenders and descenders (f, h, p).

This fun-looking font will help all kids—not just those who are dyslexic—read faster, more easily, and with fewer errors. If you want to know more about the Dyslexie font, please visit the site www.dyslexiefont.com.

The New York Times Best-Selling Series by
Henry Winkler & Lin Oliver

Here's HANK

There's a Zombie in My Bathtub

ILLUSTRATED BY SCOTT GARRETT

Grosset & Dunlap
An Imprint of Penguin Random House

To Lulu: you energize everyone you meet.
And to Stacey, always—HW

For Kiya and Teio Shimozato,
and their wonderful mom!—LO

For my Big Sis Jo,
Charlie, and Mia—SG

GROSSET & DUNLAP
Penguin Young Readers Group
An Imprint of Penguin Random House LLC

Text copyright © 2015 by Henry Winkler and Lin Oliver
Productions, Inc. Illustrations copyright © 2015 by Scott Garrett.
All rights reserved. Published by Grosset & Dunlap, an imprint of
Penguin Random House LLC, 345 Hudson Street, New York,
New York 10014. GROSSET & DUNLAP is a trademark of
Penguin Random House LLC. Printed in the USA.

Typeset in Dyslexie Font B.V.
Dyslexie Font B.V. was designed by Christian Boer.

Library of Congress Cataloging-in-Publication Data is available.

ISBN 978-0-448-48512-6 (pbk)   10 9 8 7 6 5 4 3 2 1
ISBN 978-0-448-48513-3 (hc)   10 9 8 7 6 5 4 3 2 1

CHAPTER 1

The most fun way to spend the night before Halloween is to watch a scary movie with your best friend, sharing a bowl of popcorn. This is something Frankie Townsend and I have been doing ever since I can remember. We turn out the lights in my living room and put *The Eight-Legged Creature from the Deep* on the TV. Then we make scary underwater sounds. Frankie pretends to be a giant vampire squid.

I'm really good at holding my nose and groaning. I don't think any underwater creature actually makes that noise, but I like to do it, anyway, because it drives my sister, Emily, crazy.

"Hey, Zip," Frankie said to me as we sat in the kitchen eating frozen oatmeal raisin cookies. Call me weird, but I like my cookies frozen. It was Friday night, and the next day was Halloween. "Do you think we should invite Ashley to watch the movie with us?"

"Sure," I said. "After all, she's our new best friend. Unless you think the movie would be too scary for her?"

"Let's ask her," Frankie said.

I picked up the phone and dialed Ashley's number.

"Big Joe's Hot Dogs," said a man's voice. "Where every bite is right."

Oops. I guess I didn't dial Ashley's number.

"Excuse me," I said into the phone. "I was trying to call Ashley Wong."

"No one here by that name," Big Joe answered. "But if you find her, come on in for our Halloween special. I call it the Hal-O-Wiener."

I could still hear him laughing as I hung up. Without saying a word, Frankie took the phone and dialed Ashley. He knows

I'm not the best dialer in the world. I think I've memorized a number, but when I try to dial it, all the numbers get jumbled up in my brain. I talk to a lot of nice people that way, though.

When we asked her over for the movie, Ashley said she'd love to come. She wasn't scared a bit. She just had to finish gluing the last fake diamonds on her giraffe costume, and she'd be right up.

If you're wondering why a giraffe is wearing a diamond necklace, you'll have to ask

Ashley. Hey, if it works for her, it works for me.

We had just hung up the phone when my sister, Emily, came stomping into the kitchen. She had green cardboard patches hanging all over her body.

"I give up!" She seemed ready to burst out crying. "My bony plate is coming loose again."

The kitchen door swung open, and my mom came running in after her. She was carrying a glue gun.

"Come here, Emily," she said. "I can fix your costume if you give me a minute."

"What are you supposed to be?" I asked Emily.

"Can't you tell? I am a Komodo dragon, which, in case you don't know, lives only in Indonesia."

"Are you going to move there once Halloween is over?" I shot back.

"I heard that, Hank," my dad said, joining us in the kitchen. "Don't tease Emily. Halloween is supposed to be fun. Be nice to each other."

"No problem, Dad," I said. Then, putting on my best smile, I said to Emily, "How wonderful that you won't need to wear a mask because you already look like a dragon."

"Hank, what did I just say?" my dad snapped. "You owe your sister an apology."

"Fine," I said. "Emily, I'm so sorry that I think your face looks like a dragon."

Frankie couldn't hold it in any longer, and he cracked up.

I knew we had to get out of there fast, or else I'd be grounded until next February.

We bolted for the living room to set up for movie night.

Ashley arrived at exactly seven o'clock. Frankie and I had already gotten out our copy of *The Eight-Legged Creature from the Deep*.

"You're going to love this movie, Ashweena," I said. "Especially the part where the creature gets mad and slaps the water so hard, he makes a tidal wave."

"I've seen that movie," Ashley said. "It's not really that scary. I have a better idea."

Reaching into her bag, she pulled out another movie and handed it to me.

"I say let's watch *Attack of the Zombies*," she suggested.

I glanced at the cover. Two pale, dead-looking zombies were marching toward a house. Inside, a family looked like they were screaming their lungs out.

Just looking at the picture made my hands start to sweat. If I could barely stand to look at the cover, I could only imagine how much the movie would scare me.

"I don't know," I said, shaking my head. "Zombies give me the creeps. The way they walk around moaning and eating human knees and everything." A shiver ran down my spine.

"I vote for Ashley's movie," Frankie said. "I think it'd be good for us to change things up, Zip."

"Frankie, do you remember that zombie book Ms. Finnigan read to us in the library?"

"Yeah. *The Mystery of the Zombie Cave*. It was cool."

"Maybe for you, but that story gave me bad dreams all week. I had to sleep on the floor in my mom and dad's room."

"We were in first grade then," Frankie said. "You were just a little kid. Little kids always get scared."

I didn't know how to tell Frankie that the thought of that story still made the hair on the back of my neck stand straight up.

"Besides," Frankie continued, "Ashweena and I are right here with you. We won't let any zombies eat you, will we, Ash?"

"Maybe just a toe or two," Ashley said with a laugh.

"You don't need all ten toes, anyway."

"Okay," I said, trying to join in the joke. "The way my feet smell, no zombie would want to nibble on my toes, anyway."

"That's the Hank Zipzer I know," Frankie said, slapping me on the back. "Funny. Cool. Not afraid of anything. Right, dude?"

"Right," I said. But my brain was screaming, *Not right! Not right! Not right!*

CHAPTER 2

FIVE EXCUSES I COULD USE TO GET OUT OF WATCHING THE ZOMBIE MOVIE

BY HANK ZIPZER

1. I have to go wash my hair. I think I forgot to use shampoo the first time.

2. I have to go wash my dog Cheerio's hair. I KNOW he forgot to use shampoo.

3. I have to finish my homework. (Wait, they won't believe that. I never finish my homework!)

4. The Mets called. They want me to play first base. (No, I mean they actually want me to BE the first base.)

5. I'm too scared to watch the zombie movie. (I can't say that. It makes me feel like a first-grader.)

CHAPTER 3

Before I could get up the nerve
to use even one of those excuses,
movie night had started. Ashley
took the pillows from the couch
and arranged them on the floor
for us. Frankie got the movie all
set up in the TV. Cheerio settled
in on my dad's chair, panting hard
like he does when he gets excited.
And my dad surprised us by
bringing in a big bowl of popcorn.
Emily, still half covered with
scales, followed him.

"Even though I'm not allowed to watch the movie with you, I helped Dad make you popcorn," she said. "Just to show you how nice us Komodo dragons are."

"Wow, Mr. Z," Frankie said. "That's a whole lot of popcorn."

"We made extra," my dad said, "because Nick McKelty is coming over to watch the movie with you guys."

Did he just say Nick McKelty, the biggest bully in our class, was coming over? To my apartment? That wasn't possible. My ears must have gone out for a walk.

"Wait, Dad . . . none of us invited him."

"I ran into his father on the

street," my dad explained. "He and I are going to the neighborhood-council meeting tonight. He needs a place for Nick to stay for a couple of hours. Since your mom will be home, I said of course he's welcome here."

"No, he isn't," I said loudly.

"Yes, he is," my father said, even louder.

This night was getting worse by the second. The doorbell rang, and my stomach flipped like a pancake on the griddle.

"Please, Dad," I begged. "Tell him we moved."

"Yeah," Frankie chimed in. "To Iceland."

"No," Ashley added. "To Pluto. It's the planet farthest away."

"Pluto is no longer a planet," Emily the know-it-all dragon said. "It is now known as a dwarf planet, and, if you'd like, I can explain to you why."

"You know what, Em?" I said. "Why don't you save that for a rainy day?"

The doorbell rang again.

"Fine," Emily said. "Have a good time with McKelty. Mom and I will be in my room working on my costume."

She stomped out, leaving a trail of green cardboard scales behind her. My dad picked them up as he went to open the front door. Standing in the doorway, shoving a jelly donut in his mouth, was Nick McKelty.

"I have arrived," he grunted, with the red jelly from the donut squirting through his teeth. "Now the party can finally start."

My dad got his jacket, yelled good-bye, and disappeared into the hallway with Mr. McKelty. Nick the Tick marched his blobby self into the living room and plopped down on the pillows.

"What are we watching?" he asked, stuffing the last of the donut into his mouth while his other hand was reaching for popcorn. I wondered if he was going to wipe his jelly-covered fingers on the couch pillows.

He wiped them on his pants instead.

"*Attack of the Zombies*," Frankie told him.

"That movie is for babies," he said with

a snort. "I've seen it eighty times."

"Then maybe you don't want to stay," I said. "You could hang out with Emily. She's having a dragon party in her room. You'd fit right in."

"Your family is so weird," McKelty said. "Let's just watch this movie already so I don't have to listen to you guys."

"That's a good idea," Ashley said. "Why don't you sit up on the couch so we don't have to look at the jelly hanging off your nose?"

Ashley pressed the PLAY button, and the movie started. As soon as he heard the scary music, Cheerio started to whimper. Inside, I was whimpering right along with him.

I hate scary music. I tried to hum a tune inside my head to drown it out, but the only one I could think of was "Five Little Monkeys Jumping on the Bed." That got too annoying, so I had to stop. And then, there it was again, that creepy music.

Cheerio jumped off my dad's chair and ran into Emily's room. Even though I have no interest in cardboard lizard scales, I wanted so badly to go with him. But Ashley was grinning at me and shooting me a big thumbs-up sign. She really wanted me to love this movie. I decided I'd try.

But not for long!

In the very first scene, a bunch of zombies missing hunks of their faces marched into the town. With their arms stretched out in front of them, their low moans sounded like a herd of sick cows.

I closed my eyes so I wouldn't have to see their moldy faces.

"Hey, Zipperbutt, you're not afraid, are you?" McKelty said with his usual mean laugh.

"Of course not! Why would you think I'm afraid?"

"Because you're covering your eyes."

"Oh, one of my eyelashes fell out. They do that sometimes."

I wasn't sure if he believed the excuse or not. We went back to watching the movie. By now, the zombies had reached a house and were banging on the front door. The family inside was screaming. I couldn't take it. Before I could stop myself, I crawled under the coffee table and pressed my head into the rug.

"What's your problem?" McKelty asked me.

"Oh, I dropped a piece of popcorn," I said. "Just looking for it."

"You eat floor food?" he said.

"Five-second rule," I shot back.

"I always knew you were gross, Zipperbutt, but that's *super* gross."

"You should talk, McKelty," Frankie said. "You're the one whose mouth always looks like a garbage bin."

McKelty wasn't offended by that. He just stuffed another handful of popcorn in his mouth like a hungry hog.

To my relief, the zombies couldn't break into the house

so they turned away and left
the family alone. I relaxed just
a tiny bit. Maybe these were
nice zombies. Maybe they were
just taking a nice walk in the
countryside. But then came the
part with the goat. The music
suddenly got high and screechy.
I knew something terrible was going
to happen to that poor little goat.
My heart started to beat like it
was going to fly out of my chest.

I can't tell you what happened
next, because I jumped to my feet
and ran out of there as fast as
I could. I thought I heard Ashley
calling after me, but I didn't turn
around. I ran into the bathroom
and slammed the door shut.

Okay, I confess. I did do a
quick check in the bathtub to see
if there were any zombies lurking.
There weren't. I guess they were
all in the TV. I took a deep
breath and splashed some cold
water on my face.

What's wrong with you, Hank?
I said to myself. *It's only a movie.*
Myself didn't answer. It just
felt scared.
There was a knock on the door.

"Zip," I heard Frankie's voice say. "Everything okay in there?"

"Sure, fine. No problem. Why do you ask?"

"Well, you've been in there a pretty long time. We stopped the movie to wait for you."

"Oh, you don't have to do that for me." I tried to sound calm. Frankie was my best friend. Why couldn't I just tell him that the movie was too scary for me? There was nothing wrong with that. People get scared. It doesn't mean you're a chicken.

I opened my mouth to tell him. And here's what came out.

"Be right there, Frankie."

When I went back into the

living room, Ashley whispered, "Are you okay, Hank? You want us to turn off the movie?"

Yes I did. There was my chance. But McKelty butted in and answered for me.

"We're just getting to the good part," he said. "I don't want to miss the blood and guts!"

So I sat there with my eyes half closed for the rest of the movie. I tried to focus on my mom's painting of a bowl of lemons that hung above the TV. Every time there was a zombie attack, I stared harder and harder at those lemons. Pretty soon, even they started to look like zombies to me—dripping yellow faces with rotting skin.

I was so happy when the movie finally ended. What I didn't know was that it was just the beginning of a night filled with terror.

CHAPTER 4

When I went to bed that night, I closed my eyes like I usually do. But instead of dreaming about me hitting a home run for the Mets, my brain went to Zombieland. I'm going to leave out a lot of the scariest parts of my nightmare because I don't want you to close this book and run away screaming. But here are some highlights.

In my dream, I was about five years old. I was at the beach,

building a sand castle when a
bunch of zombies came out of
the ocean. They had jellyfish for
noses, and instead of arms, they
had giant octopus tentacles. With
stingers on the end of each one!
I screamed and ran down the
beach. The zombies chased me.
As they got closer, I could almost
feel their tentacles stinging me.
One of them actually wrapped
itself around my arm and started
to squeeze.

I used every bit of my strength
to break free. I ran for the
lifeguard shack, but the faster
I ran, the farther away it got.

Then I fell facedown in the
sand. The sand got up my nose

and I couldn't breathe. I felt a cold slimy tentacle wrap around my ankle, and start pulling me— closer . . . closer . . . closer . . .

And then I woke up. I was screaming, "Let me go! Let me go!"

That woke up Frankie. He had been asleep in his Spider-Man sleeping bag next to my bed.

"Zip, what are you doing?" he said with a yawn.

"Running from a zombie attack."

"That's nice," he said, still half asleep. "Did they eat your brains?"

"I don't think so. I'm still here."

I reached up to my head to check if there were any zombie bite marks. There weren't. I leaned down to show Frankie, but he had already fallen back asleep.

I rolled back in bed and closed my eyes. As soon as I did, there they were again!

Zombies . . . hundreds of them—
pounding on the hot sand with
their tentacles. The terrible
drumming sound got louder and
louder in my ears. My eyes flew
open.

It was late, and I was so
tired. But there was no way I
could fall asleep. Not with all
those zombies in my room. It
was going to be a long, hard
night.

CHAPTER 5

I must have eventually fallen
asleep because when I opened my
eyes, it was light out. I checked
my room to make sure that it was
zombie-free. Everything was in
its place, except for Frankie. His
sleeping bag was empty. Oh no! Did
the zombies get *him* instead of *me*?

I jumped out of bed and called
out his name. But there was no
answer. Slowly, I tiptoed across the
carpet. The movie last night said
that zombies are attracted to loud

41

noises, so I wanted to be extra special quiet. I opened the door to my room and looked down the hall. It was empty. I counted to three and ran as fast as I could into the bathroom. I breathed a sigh of relief.

"Hank," I whispered to myself. "Your imagination has gone wild. This is not a movie. This is real life and you're in your real bathroom. With real toothpaste and a real shower curtain that I'm going to check again now."

I grabbed the curtain and pulled it all the way to one side.

"*Aaagggghhhhhhhhhhhhhhhh!*" I screamed at the top of my lungs.

There, in my real bathtub was

a real zombie. His face was green.
His lips were green. And his body
was covered in torn rags. He let
out a long, low moan.

"*Haaaaaaaaank*," he groaned
over and over. "*Haaaaaaaaaaaank*."

I almost jumped out of my pajamas without unbuttoning them. I opened my mouth to scream, and nothing came out. Well, something came out. It was a little chunk of last night's dinner. I wasn't going to stay around long enough to clean it up. I turned on my heels and bolted for the hall.

"Zip," a familiar voice said. "It's just me, Frankie."

"Frankie!" I wheeled around to look at him. "Did they get you, too? Are you a zombie?"

Frankie laughed and stood up in the bathtub.

"It's just me in my Halloween costume," he answered. "I had it in my bag, so I thought I'd test it out for trick-or-treating tonight. Looks like it worked."

I wanted to tell Frankie that his little test had scared me so much that my whole forehead had broken out in a cold sweat. But I was ashamed to admit that the zombie movie had gotten to me.

"Tell the truth," Frankie said, climbing out of the bathtub. "I had you believing I was a real zombie, didn't I?"

"No way," I answered, using my coolest voice. "I knew it was you all along."

I heard small feet stomping down the hall. Then a hiss. It could only be Emily. No one else in my family walks like an elephant and wears a hissing iguana around her neck like a scarf.

"Hi, Frankie," she said as she came into the bathroom, not even blinking at his zombie costume.

Wait a minute. Emily is younger than me, and she wasn't scared for one single second by Frankie's zombie-ness. What was wrong with me?

"Hank, Papa Pete's on the phone for you," Emily said. "He wants to make a plan for today—although I don't get why anyone would want to spend the day with you. I'd rather spend the day with a banana peel."

That was such a weird thing to say, I didn't even know how to answer her. So instead, I just made like a banana peel and slid all the way to the phone.

"Hankie, my boy," Papa Pete said. I could hear the smile in his voice. "How's your throwing arm today? Are you in the mood to go to the park and have a little pre— trick-or-treat catch?"

"Sure, Papa Pete. But I had

a bad night's sleep, so I don't know how good I'll be."

"You don't have to be good. We're just going to have fun together. I've got my karate class this morning, so I'll come by after lunch."

"Okay," I said. Then just before I hung up, I added, "Papa Pete, you don't think there are going to be any zombies in the park, do you?"

"Zombies?" He sounded surprised at my question.

"Yeah. Like the living-dead kind of zombies. The ones whose faces hang off their chins."

"Oh, those zombies," he said with a laugh. "Well, you never know. There might be one or two around. But if we don't yell, they won't bother us. I hear they're attracted to noise."

I hung up the phone and gulped. I think Papa Pete was kidding, but then again, he did say "You never know."

When I went back to my room, Frankie was folding up his costume and getting ready to go home.

"So, Zip," he said. "Are you still going as a kitchen sink tonight? I can lend you my plastic faucet that sticks on your forehead with a suction cup. It came with my magic set."

"I just changed my mind. I'm going as a zombie fighter."

"What exactly is that?"

"A guy who fights zombies."

"Using what, exactly?"

"I don't know yet. As soon as you leave, I'm going in the kitchen to put together my anti-zombie gear."

Frankie left, and I got busy. I went through every drawer and cabinet, picking out anything that looked like it could be used for protection against a zombie attack. An egg beater. A couple of wooden spoons. A clump of garlic to wear around my neck. A frying pan. I used the belt of my terry-cloth robe to hang all the anti-zombie gear around my waist. As a final touch, I wrapped my chest in tinfoil

so a zombie couldn't detect
my body heat.

I checked my costume out in
the mirror. If I do say so myself,
I looked very prepared. And even a
little bit scary. A guy most zombies
wouldn't want to mess with.

Not that there's any such thing
as zombies, of course.

CHAPTER 6

After lunch, I threw on my Mets baseball sweatshirt and went downstairs to wait for Papa Pete. (I should mention here that I also put on pants and sneakers. I don't want you to think I was standing in the lobby with only a sweatshirt on.)

Papa Pete arrived with two black-and-white cookies for us, and we set out for Riverside Drive Park. I tucked my baseball glove under my arm while I ate the chocolate part of the cookie first. By the time we reached the park, the only thing left was the icing on my fingers.

We found a place on the grass right next to the basketball courts. Papa Pete tossed me the ball, and I caught it, no problem. It wasn't hard because I was really close to him.

"Back up, Hankie," he said after a few minutes. "I'm going to toss you some heat."

"Not too fast, Papa Pete," I said, being careful to keep my voice down. "You know my eyes and my hands are not always friends."

"Why are you whispering?" he asked me.

"Oh, no reason." I shrugged.

"This wouldn't have anything to

do with . . . oh . . . zombies, could it?" He raised one eyebrow.

I laughed, a little too hard. Okay, way too hard.

"You've got to be kidding me," I said.

Papa Pete nodded. I think he knew what I was really scared of. Papa Pete always knows everything about me.

"Well, we're here to have fun, so let's do it," he said. "Just back up a little more, Hankie. Every couple of throws you can back up another step. Pretty soon, you'll be catching and throwing like a Major Leaguer."

We tossed the ball back and forth. I dropped some of the balls.

To be honest, I dropped most of them. But Papa Pete didn't mind. He just smiled and said, "Good try."

I took another few steps back, and Papa Pete threw me a real smoker. He has a good arm for a grandpa. Just as I stretched up in the air to catch it, I heard a mean-sounding voice shout, "I got this one, Zipperbutt."

From out of nowhere, Nick McKelty had zoomed right in front of me. Where had he come from? He held his claw-like hand up in the air and snagged the ball just before it reached my glove.

"That's how you catch a ball, ding-dong," he snarled.

"Excuse me, young man," Papa Pete called to him. "My grandson and I are having a catch here."

"You call this having a catch?" McKelty snickered. "I call it tossing around meatballs."

"Who brought you here?" Papa Pete asked, giving Nick a stern eye.

"My dad. We just came from

checking out his new bowling alley. It's going to have one hundred fifty lanes. Oh and did I mention, the balls glow a million different colors. It's so bright, you can bowl in the dark."

"Are you sure you're not making some of this up?" Papa Pete asked him.

I wanted to blurt out that McKelty was nothing but a big bully and a liar. But I didn't want to raise my voice in case of zombies.

"I've heard about this new bowling alley," Papa Pete said. "In fact, I've been looking forward to starting a bowling league in the neighborhood. Maybe I'll go discuss it with your father."

"My dad's over there on the basketball court," McKelty said. "He's the one making all the slam dunks."

"Actually, he's the short guy who keeps dropping the ball," I told Papa Pete.

"Why don't you two boys toss the ball around while I talk with your dad," Papa Pete said. "I'll be back before you can say 'Peter Piper picked a peck of pickled peppers.'"

"Why would I want to say that?" McKelty said. Obviously the big lug had never heard of Mother Goose.

Papa Pete walked over to the basketball court. Instead of

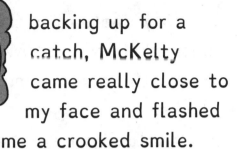

backing up for a catch, McKelty came really close to my face and flashed me a crooked smile.

"So, Zipperhead, you almost wet your pants last night, didn't you?"

"I don't know what you're talking about, Nick."

"I saw you covering your eyes during *Attack of the Zombies*. You were so scared, I thought you were going to cry. I bet you had zombie dreams, too."

"Who told you that?"
I frowned, making my voice sound angry just like my dad's does when he looks at my report card.

"I know these things," McKelty said.

"You don't know anything!" I insisted. "I wasn't scared."

"That's good, Zipperbutt, because I wouldn't want you to be afraid of that old zombie sitting on the bench over there."

My eyes darted to the park bench. A very wrinkled man was sitting there eating a brown banana. A large bandage covered one eye and part of his face.

"That's One-Eyed Gilbert," McKelty whispered in my ear. "The bandage is holding his face on. If you take it off, his eye falls out and his cheek slides right off his face."

The man's face did seem kind
of grey and loose. I didn't want
to believe McKelty, but I could
feel myself shivering, and it wasn't
even cold out.

"He's getting ready for tonight,"
McKelty went on. "The zombies
always come out on Halloween.
When they catch you, they bite

you. And then you turn into one of them."

"Everyone?" I asked. He nodded.

"Everyone they can catch. They especially like old people. They always go for them first."

A woman pushing a baby stroller walked by. The baby was crying.

"See that baby?" McKelty whispered. "I happen to know his real name is Meatbag, but they call him Zoms for short. He's a baby zombie.

Their bite is the worst. Their little baby teeth are sharp as needles."

Before I could answer, the baby picked up his bottle and threw it right at me. It hit me in the elbow.

"Oh no, he's tagged you," McKelty whispered. "You better watch out. And watch out for that grandpa of yours, too. He's an easy target."

The baby's mom asked if I would pick up the bottle and hand it to her. I didn't want to touch it, just in case it had zombie cooties. So I picked up a stick and shoved the bottle toward her.

"Where are your manners?"
she said. I didn't answer her.
I couldn't. I was busy staring at
her zombie baby. She picked up
the bottle herself and quickly
pushed the stroller away from us.

I looked around for Papa
Pete. He was just leaving the
basketball court and walking over
to us.

"Careful," Nick the Tick said, pointing to a skinny black dog that was lying under a nearby tree. "You don't want to go near him. Zombie dogs are bad news."

"Zombie dogs? I didn't know there was such a thing," I heard myself saying.

"They're the worst. They don't care what kind of brains they eat. Squirrel. Spider. I bet that guy is just about to pounce on the next squirrel he sees."

Suddenly, the dog jumped to its feet and started to bark at a little squirrel in the tree. I could see his black gums and sharp teeth.

"It's okay, boy," I tried to

whisper, but my voice cracked
with fear.

The dog turned to me, and his
bark changed into a growl. A low
growl that sounded like a moan.
A zombie moan.

I started to shake all over.

CHAPTER 7

By the time Papa Pete reached me, I was totally frozen with fear.

"Whoa there, Hankie," he said, throwing his big strong hand on my shoulder. "What's gotten into you?"

"That d-d-dog," I stammered. "He wants to eat spider brains. Or squirrels. Or maybe even mine!"

"Oh, you mean Dexter," Papa Pete said. "No way. He just likes to relax under the tree and bark at the squirrels. He's here every day."

As Papa Pete talked, I noticed

that the dog had stopped barking. I let myself turn around and look at him. He wasn't chasing me. In fact, his tail was wagging. I looked at McKelty, who had a huge grin on his thick face.

"You lied," I said to him. "That dog isn't a zombie."

"Oh yeah?" he whispered. "Just wait until dark and his eyes start to glow. You'll see what I mean."

With that, McKelty walked toward the basketball courts.

"Now what is this all about?" Papa Pete asked.

I opened my mouth and all my fear came out in one giant wave of words.

"McKelty said that tonight

there's going to be a huge zombie invasion. And that Meatbag is going to attack you. Papa Pete, what if zombies take over the city? What if they live in my building? What if they're in my bed right now, just waiting for me to come home?"

Papa Pete held up his hand.

"Okay, let's take a deep breath and just slow down here," he said. "First of all, zombies are make-believe. They don't really exist, except in stories and movies and TV."

"But, Papa Pete," I argued. "Nick McKelty pointed out three zombies right here in the park. One guy's face was being held on by just a bandage."

Papa Pete looked at me and scratched his chin.

"I can see that I'm not going to talk you out of this very easily," he said. "So I have a wonderful idea. Let's go to the library."

"Great idea!" I said. "I'll bet libraries are zombie-free zones. It's probably hard for them to read when their eyes are sliding out."

"Boy oh boy, your imagination is really flying," Papa Pete said. "But I have a cure for that."

"Do I take it with a spoon?"

"No, it's called facts, Hankie. The best cure for fear is to have the facts, nothing but the facts. I say, let's go to the library and look up zombies. I think real facts will calm you down and make you feel better."

I held Papa Pete's hand tight. We left the park and headed up 78th Street past my apartment building. At Amsterdam Avenue, we turned left and walked the two blocks to the library.

"I love this place," Papa Pete said, holding the big wooden door open for me. "It's got the delicious smell of books."

"I like the smell of books, too," I said. "I just wish they weren't so hard for me to read. It's fun to check them out with my library card, but then when I get them home, they scare me. Which reminds me—can we look up zombies, please? Right now?"

Papa Pete walked me up to the desk where a woman was sitting on a high stool, wearing a T-shirt that said, *Open a book, open your mind*. In front of her was a sign that read: MS. LOPEZ, HEAD LIBRARIAN.

"Excuse me, Ms. Lopez," Papa Pete said in his quiet library voice. "Can you help us find some information about zombies?"

"Of course I can," she answered. "They don't call me Info to Go for nothing. Follow me."

She took us to the research section on the second floor.

"You can find the history of zombies in the encyclopedia," she said. "Would you like to read that on the computer screen or in the actual book?"

"My grandpa says that books smell delicious," I said. "So I'll go for the book."

Ms. Lopez pulled out the *Z* volume of the encyclopedia and put

it on the reading table. She opened it to ZOMBIE, and then turned to Papa Pete.

"While your grandson is reading, is there something special I can help you find?"

"Well, I was just thinking about starting a bowling league. Do you happen to have the official bowling league handbook?"

"Of course, it's in the sports section. Let me show you."

"Hankie, I'll be two shelves over in the sports section," Papa Pete said. "Call if you need me."

They left. I looked down at the small print on the encyclopedia page. There were so many words there. All of a sudden, they looked like little fish swimming around in a tank of water. But if I was going to find out the truth about zombies, I had to start somewhere. No one was watching me, so I used my finger to follow every word across the page. I began to read.

"*The word* zombie *was first used in 1819 in Brazil,*" the letters said.

I was doing fine reading until that last word, the one that started with a capital *B*. I couldn't sound it out. What could it be? Bug hill? That didn't make sense. Bugs don't use words. Maybe it was Bad Bill? I wondered if he was a zombie.

Okay, Hank, I thought to myself. *You're not getting that B word, so let's just go to the next sentence.* Moving my fingers under each word, I read this.

"*According to experts, there is evidence that zombies exist.*"

Wait! What did that say? It said that zombies exist. In other words, they're real. Right there in black and white. On the page. In the actual encyclopedia. In the New York Public Library. It said that zombies are real!

With shaking hands, I slammed the book shut. I could feel my cheeks start to burn and my throat close up. I wanted to call out for Papa Pete. I opened my mouth and screamed, "Help!" but only a little squeak came out.

I looked around the room, and everyone else was just sitting there, reading their books. Like everything was normal. I was the only one who knew that tonight was the night of the real live zombie invasion.

CHAPTER 8

EIGHT THINGS I DECIDED TO DO TO PREPARE FOR THE ZOMBIE INVASION

BY HANK ZIPZER

1. Move to the Moon. (Oh, wait, there's no air there.)

2. Move to Mars. (Oh, wait, there's no air there, either.)

3. Move to France. (Oh, wait, I don't know the French word for black-and-white cookie.)

4. Move to the North Pole. (Oh, wait, my winter jacket is at the dry cleaners.)

5. Move to Hawaii. (Oh, wait, Emily wants to go there, so I'd have to take her. Forget that!)

6. Move Cheerio and me to the basement. (Oh, wait, that's the first place the zombies would look.)

7. Hide under the couch in the living room. (Oh, wait, there's so much dust under there, I'd sneeze and give myself away.)

8. Face it, Hank. You're toast.

CHAPTER 9

Papa Pete was in a great mood when he returned with Ms. Lopez.

"This trip to the library has been very successful," he said. "I now know more about bowling leagues than any human should. How about you, Hankie? Did you learn the truth about zombies?"

"I sure did," I said.

"See what I told you?" He patted me on the shoulder. "Knowing the facts is the best way not to be afraid."

He said good-bye to Ms. Lopez and we walked downstairs and out the door onto Amsterdam Avenue. I was completely silent. You're probably wondering why I didn't tell Papa Pete the real truth I learned about zombies. This is why.

I love Papa Pete more than anyone in the world. And I knew that zombies went for old people first. It was going to be up to me to protect him. I just hadn't figured out how to do that yet. So I decided to keep quiet until I figured out a plan. The last thing I wanted was to scare him, too.

When Papa Pete dropped me off at my apartment, I said to him,

"Keep your phone close, okay?"

"Why?"

"I'm going to need to talk to you in a little while."

"Oh, you've got a secret, do you?" Papa Pete said with a wink. "I love secrets." He wasn't going to love this one, that's for sure.

"Oh, and Papa Pete," I added. "You might want to practice some of your karate moves. They could come in handy."

"This gets more interesting by the minute," he said. Then he gave me one of his giant hugs and headed for home.

When I walked into my living room, my parents were busy helping Emily into her Halloween costume.

She was in a really bad mood because her tail had fallen off.

"I told you that we put too many scales on it," my dad was telling her. "The costume just couldn't take the weight."

"Fine," Emily snapped. "Then I'm not going trick-or-treating."

"Don't be silly, honey," my mom said. "You wait all year for this night."

"A Komodo dragon without a tail is like a pizza without cheese," she said, and stomped her clawed foot so hard that one of the toenails fell off, too.

"Hank," my mom said. "Maybe you can talk Emily into going out trick-or-treating with you and your friends. I don't want her to miss a good time."

"I think I'll stay home, too," I said. "You know how I always want to support my little sister."

"When did that start happening?" my dad asked.

"A minute ago."

"What's up with you, Hank?" Emily asked. "You seem weird."

"Me? Nothing's up with me. I was just thinking that what we should do tonight is call Papa Pete and have him come over. Once he's inside the apartment, we lock all the doors and windows and don't turn on any water faucets. We'll have a fun family night, just us, locked inside. Oh, and if we want to have an even better time, we could shove the couch over to block the front door."

My mom, my dad, and Emily all stared blankly at me. But before anyone could answer, the doorbell rang.

"Nobody open that,"
I whispered.

"Of course we're going to open the door," my mom said. "It's probably Frankie and Ashley. They called a few minutes ago to say they'd meet you here to go out trick-or-treating."

"But how do you know it's them and not some creepy zombie?" I blurted out.

My father had already reached the front door and opened it. Standing there was a creepy zombie, his eyes half closed and his arms reaching out to me!

"*Haaaaaannnnnnnnnnnnnnk,*" the zombie moaned. I knew that voice. It was Frankie. Standing

behind him was Ashley. At least,
I think it was Ashley. Either that,
or a giraffe wearing a really sparkly
necklace had just walked into
my apartment.

"Frankie," I said. "You can't
just come in here and scare me like
that."

"Why not, Zip? It's Halloween.
We're supposed to be scary."

"How will I be able to tell you
from the real zombies?"

Frankie laughed.

"Wow, my costume must really
be good. Now hurry up, Zip. You're
not even in your costume yet."

"We're going to miss all the
best candy," Ashley added.

"I don't think we should go

trick-or-treating in this building," I said. "I think we should head right over to Papa Pete's."

"Oh, is there better candy in his building?" Ashley asked.

"Yes," I said. "That's exactly the reason."

Actually, the real reason was, I wanted to get to Papa Pete to protect him. "But we'll miss the full-size chocolate bars in 3B. They always run out fast," Frankie reminded me.

Frankie was right. So I went along with it. "Give me a minute," I said. "I have to make an important phone call first."

I ran into the kitchen, picked up the phone, and dialed Papa Pete's number from memory. It's the only one I never get wrong.

"Papa Pete," I said, when I heard his voice. "We're coming to you right away. It's not safe for you to be there by yourself."

"Hankie," he said. "You're not still worried about zombies, are you? I thought that was the reason we went to the library."

"Yeah, and I never told you

what I learned at the library. In the encyclopedia, it said that—"

"Hankie," Papa Pete interrupted. "There's my doorbell. It must be my first trick-or-treater. Come in!" I heard him call out.

"No!" I hollered into the phone. "Don't let anyone in. Lock your door!"

Papa Pete wasn't listening. I heard him laugh and say, "What are you supposed to be? Oh, a bumblebee princess. That's so clever." Then speaking into the phone, he said to me, "Hankie, come whenever you want, but I have to go now. I've got a plastic pumpkin full of candy to hand out."

Click. Just like that, the phone went dead. I didn't even have time to tell him that the zombies were going after him first.

That did it. I had no choice. I was going to have to get trick-or-treating in our building over with as fast as possible. Then I'd make everyone trick-or-treat all the way over to Papa Pete's apartment building. I couldn't let myself be stopped by the zombie invasion.

I had to save Papa Pete.

CHAPTER 10

As I hung up the phone, the door to the kitchen swung open, and Frankie stuck his head in.

"We really have to go, Zip. Do you need help with your costume?"

"Actually, I do. I can tie on my anti-zombie gear, but I could use some help with the tinfoil."

"*Okaaaay*," Frankie said, raising his eyebrows. "I'm your tinfoil man."

I took out the terry-cloth robe belt that had all the stuff hanging off it and tied it around my waist.

Then I went to the second drawer under the sink where my mom keeps the sandwich bags and stuff like that. I pulled out the roll of tinfoil and handed it to Frankie.

"Wrap me up," I said. "You pull the tinfoil off the roll and I'll turn. Don't stop until I'm completely wrapped up like a hot dog at a Mets game."

My idea was that if no zombie could pick up my body heat, they would pass me right by. I wasn't sure if it would work, but it was worth a try. Anything to get safely to Papa Pete's.

Frankie and I worked quickly. In a few minutes, I was wrapped in tinfoil from head to toe, except for my nose and mouth and eyes.

"Actually, you look pretty cool," Frankie said, standing back to admire his work. "Let's go ring some doorbells."

"Okay," I said. "But we have to hurry so we can get to Papa Pete's soon."

"What's the rush?" Frankie asked. "Afraid they'll run out of candy in his building?"

"You never know," I answered.

I hurried into the living room. You could hear the tinfoil crinkle as I took each step. Emily let out a huge laugh when she saw me.

"What are you supposed to be? A tuna sandwich in a lunch bag?"

"Can we just go?" I snapped.

"Okay, I've decided to go with you," Emily said. "Even my broken dragon costume doesn't look as bad as yours."

"I'll come with you kids," my dad said. "Mom will stay here to hand out candy."

"Oh, I don't believe in unhealthy snacks," my mom said. "I'm handing out little boxes of raisins."

Normally, I would have told my mom that raisins are for putting in cereal and not for Halloween treats. But I was in a rush to get going, so I just said, "Great idea, Mom. And please check to make sure everyone you open the door for is actually alive!"

We left the apartment and went across the hall. The first doorbell we rang was apartment 10B where Dr. James Watson and his family live. The Watsons had just moved in a couple weeks before, so we didn't know him very well.

"Trick or treat," Emily growled, trying to sound like what a Komodo dragon would sound like if it spoke English.

"Trick or treat," Frankie and Ashley chimed in.

"Oh my," Dr. Watson said as he opened the door. "What have we here? A zombie, a sparkly giraffe, a roll of tinfoil, and a dragon with a missing tail."

Emily looked down on the floor, and saw that her tail had completely fallen off once again. She burst into tears, picked up her tail, and stomped back toward our apartment.

"I'll go with her and do an

emergency repair," my dad said. "You kids stay on this floor until I'm back."

Dr. Watson held out a bowl of candy. It was filled with whole candy bars, not the fun-size ones. Ashley and Frankie started to sort through all the different candy bars to pick their favorite one.

"Hurry up, guys," I whispered. "We have to move faster than this."

A little boy in a Superman cape and red rain boots came running to the door.

"Look, Daddy," he said, pointing at me. "He looks like a sandwich in my lunch box."

"That he does, Luke,"

Dr. Watson agreed. "Have you kids met my son, Luke?"

"I'm not Luke, I'm Super Luke," he said.

"Well, Super Luke," I said to him. "Just so you know, I am not something you eat. I am a zombie-detecting robot."

Luke's eyes grew wide.

"Zombies!" Luke screamed. "I hate zombies!"

And he ran as fast as he

could back into his apartment.

"I better go now," Dr. Watson said, closing the door on us. "Thanks for coming by, kids."

Boy, did I know how little Super Luke felt. I hated zombies, too.

All of a sudden, I heard the elevator *ding* as it arrived on our floor. I stepped out in front of Frankie and Ashley.

"Hide behind me," I whispered. "It might be THEM."

"Who?" Ashley whispered back.

"*Shhhhhhhhhhh*. Say nothing."

The elevator door creaked as it slid open. I held my breath and waited to see who was coming out.

Please don't be a zombie, I thought.

It wasn't a zombie. At least,
it wasn't one we could see. No
one was in the elevator. Then why
did it come to our floor? Was it
THEM, sending us a message? Was
Meatbag the baby zombie coming
to find me?

The elevator door slid shut.

"That was creepy," I whispered.

"Zip, it was just an empty elevator," Frankie said. "I bet that Robert Upchurch from the fourth floor pushed every button. He's the kind of kid who'd think that was funny."

Ashley had already rung the doorbell of apartment 10C where Mrs. Fink, a very nice older lady, lives.

The door flew open and out of it burst a bright green face and a deep hole where the mouth should be. There were no lips. There were no teeth. Just loose skin the color of green slime.

"*Helloooooooo*, kids," the face cackled. It almost sounded like

Mrs. Fink, but I knew it wasn't. She had been turned into a zombie! McKelty was right. They had gone for the old people first!

"Run!" I screamed.

"Run?" Frankie said. "But she's got Tootsie Rolls!"

I grabbed Frankie by the arm and yanked him toward the door of my apartment.

"You too, Ashley," I screamed, "before that horrible green zombie eats your brain!"

I was already banging on the door of our apartment, wildly turning the knob trying to get it open.

"Help, Mom!" I yelled. "Open the door."

But it was too late. The slimy green hand touched my shoulder, and the creature pulled me toward her. And then that scary, awful zombie let out a wicked laugh.

CHAPTER 11

The door to our apartment opened just in time. I had never been so glad to see my mom's face. I broke free from the zombie and zoomed inside like I had a jet pack on my back.

"Frankie! Ashley! Get in here," I yelled. "And Mom! Slam the door! Quick!"

But my mom wasn't fast enough, and the green-faced zombie followed us into the living room. This was it. I had no choice.

It was time for me to be brave.

"Stop right there," I said, stepping in front of my family and friends and spreading my tinfoil arms in front of them. "I am a zombie fighter. Take one step farther and I'll have to use my powers to melt you into a green puddle."

"Hank," my mom said. "That's no way to talk to Mrs. Fink."

"But, Mom, can't you see? That's not really Mrs. Fink anymore. She's been taken over by zombies. Just look at her."

"Oh," Mrs. Fink said, reaching out to touch my arm. "I think I understand the problem."

"Don't get near me," I warned

her. "You can't eat my brain. It's off-limits."

"I'm not a zombie, honey," she said. "I promise."

"Then why is your face green?"

"I was just having some Halloween fun. So I covered my face with my avocado face cream."

"Oh really? Then where have your teeth gone?"

"They're in a glass on the sink. Maybe you didn't know, but I wear false teeth. I'm so sorry that I scared you."

"Mrs. Fink," my mom said. "I'm so embarrassed about the way Hank spoke to you. If you'll excuse us, I'd like to have a word with him."

Mrs. Fink winked at me as she left, and a big glob of green slime slid off her face onto her shoes.

"Don't forget to come back for a Tootsie Roll," she said to all three of us as she left our apartment.

My mom looked me right in the eye.

"What is all this about, Hank?" she asked.

"I think I know, Mrs. Zipzer," Ashley said. "Ever since last night's movie, Hank has been worried about a zombie invasion."

"We thought he was just

kidding," Frankie said. "But now we see he wasn't."

"This is silly, Hank," my mom said. "There's no such thing as zombies. They are made up."

"Oh yeah?" I said. "Then how come it says in the encyclopedia at the library that zombies do exist? I read it, right on the page. It said, "*According to experts, there is evidence that zombies exist.*"

My mom nodded her head.

"I think I understand what's happening here," she said slowly. "Isn't it true, sweetie, that reading is very hard for you? And sometimes you add words to what's on the page . . . or leave words out?"

"I guess that's true, Mom."

"So I suggest we all go to the computer and look up zombies again. We'll give it another reading."

Frankie, Ashley, and I followed my mom to the dining-room table, where she sat down in front of her laptop.

She typed in some words. In just a few seconds, the encyclopedia page about zombies popped up. It was the same page that was in the book I read.

Frankie leaned toward the screen and read the first sentence out loud.

"The word zombie *was first used in 1819 in Brazil,"* he read.

"Oh, that's what that word was," I said. *"Brazil!* Well, that makes much more sense than Bad Bill."

Frankie continued reading. *"According to experts, there is no evidence that zombies exist."*

"Wait a minute," I said. "Where do you see the word *no?"*

"It's right here, Zip," he said, pointing to the word on the screen.

"Do you think it was there this whole time?" I asked.

"Yes, I do."

There was a long silence as I thought about that.

"So I've been scared of a zombie invasion this whole time because I skipped over a two-letter word?"

Frankie and Ashley and my mom all nodded.

For some reason, I felt like I was going to cry. Why couldn't I read like Frankie and Ashley? At that moment, I really didn't like my brain. Why didn't it work like everyone else's?

Ashley put one of her giraffe hooves on my shoulder.

"You'll catch on to this reading thing, Hank," she said. "In the meantime, Frankie and I are here to help you."

"Does this mean we can go out trick-or-treating now?" Frankie said. "Because there's a whole lot of candy out there with our names on it."

For the first time in twenty-four hours, I was able to smile.

I was safe. My parents and Emily were safe. And best of all, Papa Pete was safe.

"Let's do it," I said.

My dad came out of Emily's room.

"Ladies and gentlemen, giraffes and zombies, may I have your attention, please?" he said in his circus-announcer voice. "Introducing the world's only Komodo dragon with an upside-down tail. Emily, if you please."

My sister came out of her bedroom looking very happy with herself. Her tail had been stapled back on, and this time, the tip of it was pointing right up to the ceiling. A string tied it to the top of her dragon head.

"The string was all my idea,"
she said proudly. "This tail will
stay on for weeks. I might even
wear it to school Monday!"

"Nothing weird about that,"
I said. "Remind me not to walk
to school with you Monday."

"So," my dad said, going to
the front door. "Are we all ready
for some trick-or-treating?"

We all cheered and headed across the living room. Then we heard it: a frightened scream coming from the hall.

"Don't eat my head," the voice wailed. "*Pleeease*, Mrs. Zombie. I'll do anything you want!"

That voice was so familiar.

"Isn't that . . . ," Ashley said.

"I think it is." Frankie nodded.

I pulled open the door. Kneeling in our hallway was a kid dressed as a hockey player, holding up his stick to protect himself from green-faced Mrs. Fink, the zombie. He had a big face and a thick neck and a huge wad of red licorice stuck between his teeth.

That's right. It was tough
guy Nick McKelty, shaking and
whining like a two-year-old.

I burst out laughing.
Somebody should tell that guy
there's no such thing as zombies.

CHAPTER 12

THREE THINGS I LEARNED FROM THIS HALLOWEEN

BY HANK ZIPZER

1. Brazil is a country.
2. Tootsie Rolls are hard to get out of your teeth.
3. Zombies do NOT really exist.
4. Oops, I was only supposed to write three. Sorry!